DEDICATION

To family loved and lost, my heart is always with you.
For my mother, my inspiration, my light, my best friend,
nothing is the same with you gone.
For my many fans… thank you for being the inspiration
that keeps me going.

Prologue

He watched her. Young. Beautiful. Her smile lit up her face with a glow that could brighten the gloomiest day. She moved with a gracefulness many in today's era lacked. A dancer. She must be a dancer. Oh, not a stripper or some slapping, clapping hoe-down dancer, or even that twerking which was the rage now-a-days, but instead, something elegant. Graceful. Her movements, even minor gestures, were too fluid and gentle. She many not make a living at it, but it was ingrained within her.

His eyes darkened as he continued to gaze upon her. He was almost sad for what would soon befall her. He didn't want to do it. Really, he didn't. A part of him, albeit a very minute part, hated what he did, but it was part of who he was. However, just as much as he abhorred what he did, it was also an extreme high he couldn't refuse. It whispered to him, beckoned him as an addict was constantly called to their addiction. It couldn't be stopped. It wouldn't be. As much as he might loathe it, he also relished the power it gave him. He never detested himself because of it. He wasn't sure he was capable of that, at least not anymore. He enjoyed the omnipotent feeling it gave him far too much.

She turned the corner and climbed the steps into a small bungalow. He rushed then, moving with a quickness that belied his physical form. He moved silently to get behind her, slipping inside before she was even aware of his presence. Without thinking, she flipped the door closed and tossed the keys on a small table beside it with a delicate clink. She flipped the hallway switch to turn on the lights, but they didn't go on. She hadn't yet realized the door hadn't fully shut, nor that he had snuck in, moving to a darkened corner so he wouldn't be immediately noticed.

It was dark. He had taken care of the lights in her house earlier so the inky blackness of a moonless night would cover the domain like a woolen blanket. Rich, almost suffocating. It was only when he slid the lock in place did she turn, sensing she wasn't alone. Her inner instinct of danger kicked into action causing a fight-or-flight response even though she wasn't quite sure the cause of her feelings, until she saw the movement of him stepping closer to her.

She opened her mouth to scream as she turned to bolt, needing to escape the intruder, but he was quicker, stronger. Dare she think it in her panic state? Almost…inhuman. The attempt she made to elude him as his hand grasped her by the throat to pull her against his bare, hairless chest was futile at best. His other hand clasped over her mouth to muffle her vocal terror. He smiled, knowing what was about to come, knowing he would enjoy every morsel she would relinquish unwillingly to him. His original, momentary hatred of what he had to do dissipated now that she was in his grip. She reeked of fear, overpowering even her heady perfume and the scent of alcohol lingering on her breath.

His eyes gazed into hers, alight with an inner glow, unnatural yet mesmerizing. She stilled her struggles within his arms, entranced as his orbs penetrated her very own, touching her soul. He released her, knowing she was totally under his control.

She didn't move, bewitched and completely under his spell. Placing his hand on her left breast, he squeezed the soft mound of flesh, watching her closely, able to see clearly despite the lack of light. He leaned in as if to kiss her. Only when he could feel her breath on his face did he speak softly, commanding her to open her mouth.

She did so without hesitation. He mimicked her gesture, inhaling deeply. A soft, white adumbration danced from her mouth into his and he greedily took it within himself, closing his eyes as her soul passed into him.

Images of her life, from the moment of being slapped by the doctor upon her birth from her mother's womb, to learning how to ride a bike, to her first day at school, up to the moment she walked in the door just minutes before flashed into his mind as he feasted upon her spirit. A part of her would be immortal as it never would have been, for now it would live within him.

It barely took fifteen minutes to relive her entire life before she was fully depleted of her eternal essence. He pulled his hand off her breast before he used super strength to bust through the cavity wall and pull her heart out. He watched her eyes widen in stunned surprise as she sank to the floor. Standing above her, he engorged himself upon her heart, his own chest now covered in splatterings and drippings of her life's blood.

Having finished his indulgence, he elongated his fingernails to razor-sharp points and leaned over her prone body. Her sightless eyes were still staring up at him. He pried out one of her eyeballs from its socket. He sucked on it for a moment, then opened up a leather pouch tied to his waist and plopped in the new addition to his ever-growing collection. He then repeated the process with the other orb.

Years ago, he used to be able to finish and leave, but with all the advances in modern technology he had to adapt with some minor cleanup, such as wiping down anything he had touched. His work complete, he removed the animal-skinned flask also tied to his waist and doused her with the contents before lighting a match. As the woman's body burned, he closed his eyes and inhaled deeply, relishing the scent of burnt flesh. A few moments later, as the fire increased with its own intensity, he walked out the door. Once more he used the rag to wipe down the prints on the handle. Once outside and away from possible prying eyes, he shifted into his animal form and departed.